HENRY HECKELBECK

Is Out of This World

By **Wanda Coven**

Illustrated by **Priscilla Burris**

LITTLE SIMON

New York London Toronto Sydney New Delhi

LITTLE SIMON

An imprint of Simon & Schuster Children's Publishing Division

1230 Avenue of the Americas, New York, New York 10020

First Little Simon paperback edition July 2022

Copyright © 2022 by Simon & Schuster, Inc.

Also available in a Little Simon hardcover edition.

All rights reserved, including the right of reproduction in whole or in part in any form. LITTLE SIMON is a registered trademark of Simon & Schuster, Inc., and associated colophon is a trademark of Simon & Schuster, Inc.

For information about special discounts for bulk purchases, please contact Simon & Schuster Special Sales at 1-866-506-1949 or business@simonandschuster.com. The Simon & Schuster Speakers Bureau can bring authors to your live event. For more information or to book an event contact the Simon & Schuster Speakers Bureau at 1-866-248-3049 or visit our website at www.simonspeakers.com.

Designed by Leslie Mechanic

Manufactured in the United States of America 0522 MTN

10 9 8 7 6 5 4 3 2 1

Library of Congress Cataloging-in-Publication Data

Names: Coven, Wanda, author. | Burris, Priscilla, illustrator. | Title: Henry Heckelbeck is out of this world / by Wanda Coven ; illustrated by Priscilla Burris. | Description: First Little Simon paperback edition. | New York : Little Simon, 2022. | Series: Henry Heckelbeck ; 9 | Summary: "Henry visits the Brewster Space Center with his class, but when his best friends think they spot a real-life alien and a real-life spaceship, Henry goes on an out-of-this-world adventure!"—Provided by publisher. | Identifiers: LCCN 2021044297 (print) | LCCN 2021044298 (ebook) | ISBN 9781665911405 (paperback) | ISBN 9781665911412 (hardcover) | ISBN 9781665911429 (ebook) | Subjects: CYAC: School field trips—Fiction. | Human-alien encounters—Fiction. | Magic—Fiction. | Friendship—Fiction. | Classification: LCC PZ7.C83393 Hqj 2022 (print) | LCC PZ7.C83393 (ebook) | DDC [Fic]—dc23 | LC record available at https://lccn.loc.gov/2021044297 | LC ebook record available at https://lccn.loc.gov/2021044298

CONTENTS

Chapter 1

WIDE AWAKE

Henry Heckelbeck wriggled from under his covers and gazed at the twinkly stars. He heard Dad's slippers *wisp* down the hallway. They stopped in front of Henry's door.

"Too excited to sleep?" Dad asked. Henry turned around. "Yup, way too excited!" he said.

In the morning Henry's class was going on a field trip to the Space Center, which had rocket ships and maybe even *aliens*.

"Have you ever been to space, Dad?" Henry asked.

Dad sat down and said, "Only in my dreams."

Henry crawled under the covers as Dad handed him a stuffed green alien.

"Maybe you'll space travel in your dreams tonight," Dad said.

Henry yawned. "If I ever fall asleep."

Dad pushed Henry's hair out of his eyes. "Pretend you're sleeping in space," he said.

Henry shut his eyes and imagined floating in space.

Dad stood up and whispered, "Night night, Space Man."

Henry rolled over.

"Night, Astro-Dad," he said before falling asleep.

Chapter 2

Henry and his best friend, Dudley Day, were the first ones on the bus.

"Guess what! Last night I spied an alien spaceship in the sky!" Dudley said.

Henry's eyes widened. "No way!"

Dudley nodded and said, "Well, I'm pretty sure, because it had a searchlight and was moving really fast."

Henry whipped out his spy notebook. "Possible alien spaceship sighted from Dudley Day's house," he spoke as he wrote.

A girl's head popped up over the back of her seat. It was Max Maplethorpe.

"Are you two talking about ALIENS?" she asked.

The boys looked at each other.

"Maybe," said Henry.

Max smiled slyly. "Do you BELIEVE in them?"

The boys rolled their eyes.

"Of course we do!" said Dudley. "We can't be the ONLY planet with life-forms!"

Max smirked and asked, "But how can you be sure?"

"Um, because scientists are looking for extraterrestrial life EVERY day," said Dudley.

Max hung her elbows over the seat. "But has a REAL alien ever landed on Earth?" she asked.

Then Henry had an idea. "We can ask the experts at the Space Center!"

Max smiled mischievously.
"You never know. Maybe I'M
an expert on aliens!" she
joked. *"Meep! Meep!"*

Chapter 3

SPACE SPIES

The Space Center had three domes that looked like planets. A telescope stuck out from the top of one of the domes.

"It's so futuristic!" exclaimed Henry.

Dudley nodded and said, "I'll bet you can see a bajillion stars through THAT telescope!"

Max popped up over her seat again. "Or a bajillion ALIENS!" she said.

The boys laughed.

Ms. Mizzle walked to the front of the bus and made an announcement. "Remember, class, no alien behavior in the Space Center! 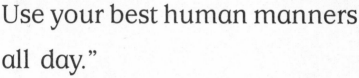 Use your best human manners all day."

Then the bus door swung open, and the kids thundered down the steps.

A man in a white lab coat and large round glasses met them at the entrance. He wore a black necktie with glow-in-the-dark moons, stars, and alien faces.

"Welcome,
Brewster
Elementary!"
he cheered.
"I'm Mr. Astro,
and I'll be
your guide to

the stars and beyond today!
Who's excited to learn about
our amazing universe?"

The class all raised their
hands and asked questions.

"Is there really a MAN in the moon?" asked Sam Sterling.

"Is the moon made of CHEESE?" asked Nina Noff.

Then Henry asked, "Will we get to see ALIENS?"

Mr. Astro laughed and said, "We'll find answers to all your questions inside, but first you will need your special space explorer badges!"

He pulled a stack of stickers from his pocket. They had a dark blue background with stars and a picture of a rocket.

"Now we're official space explorers!" said Dudley.

Henry stuck a badge on his shirt and corrected his friend. "You mean official space SPIES!"

Chapter 4

THE MYSTERY CURTAINS

The students paraded by the Space Center gift shop.

"We'll stop here on the way out," said Ms. Mizzle.

Henry and Dudley peered in the windows.

They spied astronaut flight suits, model rocket ships, and space backpacks.

Next they passed the cafeteria, which was called the Food Lab. The walls looked like outer space,

with planets, asteroids, spacecraft, and floating astronauts.

Then they cruised down the Astronaut Hall of Fame. The glass display cases had space suits worn by *real* astronauts. Another case had *real* moon rock samples.

Max ran up to the boys. "Isn't this place cool?" she asked.

They nodded excitedly.

"Look over there," Dudley said. He pointed to a pair of large curtains with a sign in front that read DO NOT ENTER. "I wonder what's going on."

"They're probably working on a new exhibit," said Henry.

Max elbowed Henry. "Or do you think they're HIDING something?" she asked.

Henry raised an eyebrow and asked, "Like what?"

"I dunno," said Max, "but a good space spy always asks questions."

Henry and Dudley looked at the curtains with new interest. At that very moment an arm reached out and pulled the curtains all the way closed.

But it wasn't just *any* arm. It was a *fuzzy green* arm with a *fuzzy green* hand.

Henry and Dudley gasped.

Had they just seen . . . an *alien*?!

Chapter 5

THE SPACE-A-TORIUM

"Attention, space explorers!" called Mr. Astro. "We're about to enter the Space-a-torium for some educational fun!"

Then he headed away from the mysterious curtain.

"Aww. This is NO time for educational fun," Henry groaned. "We have to track down an alien!"

Max wedged between the boys and slung her arms around their shoulders. "Don't worry, guys!" she said. "We can do our alien spy work at lunch."

Then she began to walk, pushing the boys along with her.

In the Space-a-torium, they watched a movie about the universe. Henry loved it so much that he almost forgot about the alien—*almost*.

When the lights came back on, the kids rubbed their eyes. "What did everyone learn?" asked Mr. Astro. He called on Nina.

"I learned that even though craters make the moon look like Swiss cheese, the moon's not actually MADE of cheese," said Nina.

Sam waved his hand in the air until Mr. Astro called on him.

"Um," Sam started, "from Earth it may look like the moon has a face, but there's no man IN the moon."

"But there has been a man ON the moon," Max added.

Then Mr. Astro called on Henry.

"The film said there are probably other life-forms in the universe," noted Henry. "And someday VERY SOON I plan to prove it."

The class cheered and giggled. Then everyone filed out of the Space-a-torium and went to the Food Lab.

"It's launch time!" cried
Henry as they sat at a table.
"Get it? LAUNCH time—instead
of LUNCH time?"

"Well, I'm not hungry," said Max.

"Me neither!" Henry agreed. "It's time to find out what's behind that curtain!"

Dudley's eyes darted from side to side. "But what about the Do Not Enter sign?"

"We're SPIES, Dudley! Not CHICKENS!" Max reminded him.

Dudley pushed back his chair and stood up. "Okay, fellow spies!" he said. "Let's go find ourselves an ALIEN!"

Chapter 6

HIDE!

The three spies slipped out of the Food Lab. Then they zipped to the mysterious curtains. They pressed their backs against the wall and sidestepped closer.

Max checked in both directions.

"Okay, Henry," she said. "GO!"

He crept to the middle of the curtains and poked his head between them. No aliens. But he *did* see something else.

"WHOA!" Henry gasped.

"What?" asked the others as they peeked behind the curtains too.

"It's a REAL spaceship!" cried Dudley.

Max pushed her way past Dudley and began to walk toward the spaceship.

"Max, what are you doing?!" Henry whisper-shouted.

She kept walking and pushed a button on the side of the spaceship.

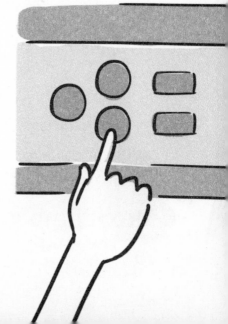

Zurr-oop! The door opened
and a walkway glided down.
Max climbed on board.

"She did NOT just do that!" said Dudley.

Henry nodded. "Yup, she definitely DID! Let's go!"

They sprinted after Max and leaped aboard the spaceship. Max was sitting at a control panel, which had a large black screen above it.

"Wow!" Henry cried as he forgot all about his worries. "This is like being inside a video game—ONLY BETTER!"

There was a big red button that pulsed with light in the middle of the control panel.

"I wonder what THAT does?" Dudley asked.

"Only one way to find out," said Max as she reached for the button.

"NO!" Henry warned.

Max laughed. "I was just kidding, Henry."

Then Dudley cried, "GUYS! Somebody's COMING!"

They all froze and listened to the sound of footsteps outside.

"HIDE!" Henry whispered
and hid beside the door.

Dudley dropped to his knees and crawled under the control panel.

Max did the unthinkable. She pushed the red button.

Chapter 7

BUTTON PUSHER!

Whoosh! The door flipped shut, and all the buttons on the control panel started blinking wildly.

Beeeeep! Whirrr! Zoooop!

The spaceship came to life.

Dudley jumped up to his feet and screamed, "What's happening?!"

"Calm down, silly," said Max. "We're just HIDING. It's not like the spaceship is going to blast off into space."

But then a pixelated face appeared on the screen and said, "Hello, space explorers! Please secure your safety belts and prepare to blast off into space."

Henry ran his hands through his hair and said, "Prepare to WHAT?!"

"We'd better buckle up!" said Max as she reached for her safety belt.

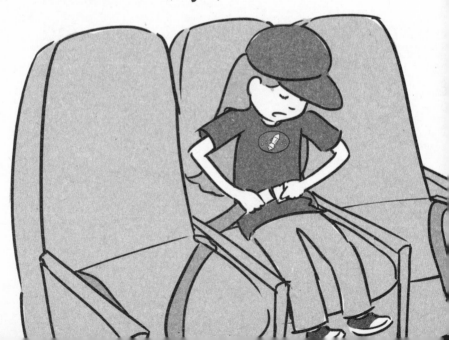

But Henry and Dudley were too busy pushing as many buttons on the control panel as they could.

"We have to stop this thing!" Dudley cried.

Henry pushed the big red button again with the heel of his hand. "Maybe this will reverse what Max did!" he said.

But instead, numbers started counting down on the screen.

"Time remaining . . . FIVE seconds," the spaceship announced. *"FIVE! FOUR!"*

Henry and Dudley stumbled
back into the seats beside Max
and strapped themselves in.
"THREE! TWO! ONE!

BLAST OFF!"

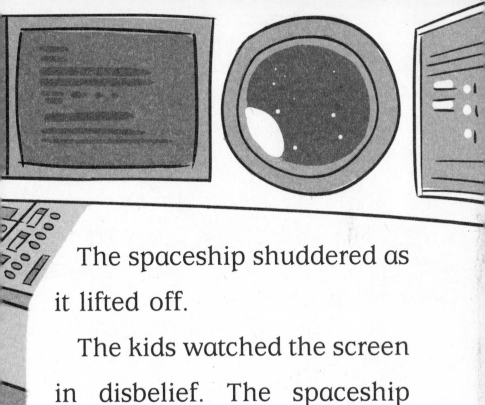

The spaceship shuddered as it lifted off.

The kids watched the screen in disbelief. The spaceship hurtled out of the Earth's atmosphere. Blue skies had given way to the darkness of outer space.

"Wow!" Max exclaimed. "The stars seem so close!"

Henry and Dudley stared at Max, who seemed to have no idea what she'd done.

"The stars ARE close!" Henry barked. "Because if you hadn't noticed, WE'RE IN OUTER SPACE!"

Chapter 8

OUT OF THIS WORLD

"Destination: the MOON!" the spaceship announced.

Dudley gulped. "Um, isn't that a little FAR from home?!"

Max giggled and covered her mouth.

"This is NOT funny!" Dudley snapped. "What if we can't get back to Earth?"

Max shrugged. "Well, we can always be space spies!"

Dudley's jaw dropped wide open. He was about to ask Max what was going on when the spaceship started talking again.

"Did you know that a million Earths could fit inside the sun?"

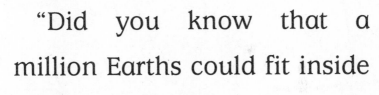

Henry smacked his head with the palm of his hand.

"No one cares, spaceship!" he screamed. "Just turn us around!"

Max studied the control panel.

"It can't be THAT hard to fly this thing," she said. "Let's see if this button helps."

Max pushed a yellow button,
and the spaceship shook and
shifted directions.

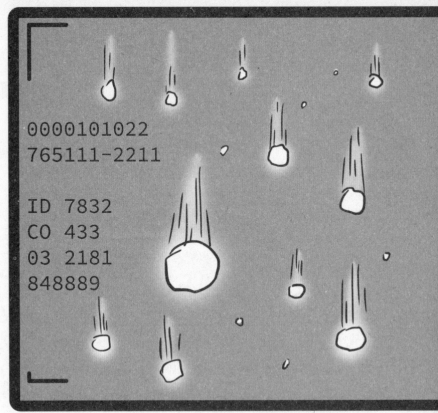

"You have now entered a meteor shower!" the spaceship said. "Meteors may cause damage to the spacecraft!"

Loud alarms started blaring in the ship. A screen lit up to show hundreds of meteors headed right for them.

"Change course!" shouted
Henry.

He shut his eyes and wished
for his magic book. The book

always showed up in times of trouble. But when Henry opened his eyes, all he saw were more meteors.

A drawer slid open next to Dudley. There was a controller inside with buttons and arrows, like a video game controller.

"Maybe we can use THIS to get home!" Dudley suggested.

"Or we could push another
button," said Max.

The boys jumped in front of
Max and said, "NO!"

The spaceship spoke up again. "Did you know the Earth is 238,900 miles from the moon?"

"BE QUIET, spaceship!" the boys shouted at the same time.

And that's when Max grabbed the controller from Dudley and pushed another button. *Za-roop!* The spaceship lurched forward—toward the meteors.

The boys covered their eyes. Max laughed again and pushed another button. The alarms stopped as the spaceship swirled and headed toward a blue-and-green planet.

"Destination: EARTH!" the spaceship announced.

Henry and Dudley sighed in relief.

"Let's just hope the space-ship goes back to Brewster," said Henry.

"Dude," Max said, "just RELAX and enjoy the ride."

Henry glanced sideways at his friend. She seemed a little TOO calm about everything.

As they reentered the Earth's atmosphere, the spaceship slowed down.

"Space explorers, prepare for landing!"

The kids gripped their safety belts, squeezed their eyes shut, and waited for touchdown.

Chapter 9

IT'S BA-A-A-ACK!

The spaceship landed with a jolt as the pixelated face appeared on the screen again.

"Welcome to Earth. And thanks for flying the cosmic skies!"

Max unclipped her harness and hopped out of her seat. "Well, THAT was a wild ride!" she said. "I mean, how could this day get weirder?"

The others got up too as the spaceship door glided open again. And there, standing in plain sight, was the fuzzy green alien.

"Oh my GOSH!" Henry whispered. "It's the alien!"

Dudley stood still, unable to move. Then he said, "We come in peace."

But Max wasn't surprised at all. Instead, she started laughing uncontrollably.

"Henry! Dudley!" she said.
"That's just my MOM!"

Henry and Dudley looked at
each other in shock.

"If that's your mom, then that means YOU'RE an alien?" asked Dudley. Now Max was rolling on the floor with a full-blown fit of the giggles.

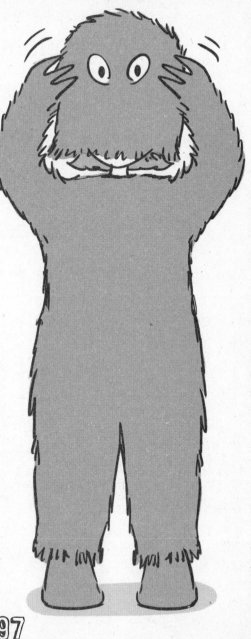

"What is going on here?" asked Henry.

Then the alien pulled off its head and revealed a blond woman who looked a lot like Max.

"I can explain," the woman said. "I actually *am* Max's mom, and I work as a scientist at the Space Center. I'm also Orbi, the Space Center's new

alien character. And this isn't a real spaceship. It's a new ride called Orbi's Orbitron. And you three were the first to ride it! What did you think?"

Max stood back up and hugged her mom. "They were both scared out of their minds!" she said.

"But it felt so REAL," said
Henry. "It was like we were
actually flying in space!"

Max's mom
smiled and said,
"Perfect! That's
the way it was
supposed to feel!"

"Since my mom works here,
we were invited to be the first
ones to try the new ride,"
Max explained.
"Everyone
knew about it
EXCEPT you guys!"

Henry shook his head. "You PLANNED this whole thing? The alien arms? The curtains? The spaceship!"

Max nodded, and Henry drew in a deep breath. "Well, thanks!" he said. "Because it was totally out of this world!"

"And super scary!" Dudley added. "I loved every minute of it!"

Then everyone laughed.

Chapter 10

SPACE PUPPETS

Henry, Dudley, and Max had gotten hungry in space. They ran back to the Food Lab and ate their lunches.

Mrs. Maplethorpe gave them alien gummies for dessert.

After lunch they joined the rest of the class in the Rocket Garden.

The class climbed inside rockets and lunar modules. Ms. Mizzle took a picture of Henry, Dudley, and Max beside a rocket.

Then the class visited the gift shop. It had space board games, space puzzles, space playing cards—even space puppets. Henry picked up an alien puppet.

"So, Max," he said, working the puppet's mouth and using an alien voice, "do you believe in aliens or not?"

Max slipped on a space monkey puppet.

"Eee! Eee! Ooo! Ooo! Ooo!" squeaked Max in space monkey talk. "I can't say for sure, but I do believe in astrobuddies, and I know one named Henry Heckelbeck, and he has a BIG secret . . . !"

Henry gulped. Did Max know about his magic?

"What kind of secret?" Henry asked with his puppet.

"Just that you're actually an alien in disguise and were sent to spy on my friend Max, the most normal human being on Earth!" Max said with her puppet.

Then Dudley slipped on an astro-bear puppet and made *it* talk.

"I don't know what's funnier, Max—that you think Henry's an ALIEN or that you think you're NORMAL!"

The three friends cracked up and flung the space puppets back in the bin.

As they lined up to get back on the bus to school, Henry held his hand out to Dudley and Max.

"Here's to space friends!" he said.

Dudley and Max piled their hands on top of Henry's.

"To space friends!" they shouted.

"And to aliens!" added Henry, putting his hand back on top.

"To ALIENS!" they shouted.

Meep! Meep!

Check out the next book starring

HENRY HECKELBECK

HENRY HECKELBECK
Chills Out

Henry Heckelbeck threw on his boots, ran out the back door, and jabbed a yardstick in the fresh snow. *Whoa! It's a whole foot deep!*

He raced back inside and

An excerpt from *Henry Heckelbeck Chills Out*

waited for his friends Dudley Day and Max Maplethorpe. They were coming over to have an epic snow day.

As soon as they arrived, Dudley and Max kicked their boots off and hung up their jackets.

Henry smiled as Dudley lifted his nose into the air.

"*Mmmm*, what smells so good?" asked Dudley.

An excerpt from *Henry Heckelbeck Chills Out*

"Mom made her Magical Hot Chocolate Special," said Henry. "Want some?"

"You bet I do!" said Dudley. "Your mom's hot chocolate is the BEST in the world!"

Mom laughed. "How do you know? You haven't had it yet!"

"Oh, Henry pinkie swears it's the BEST," Max cheered.

"Really? A pinkie swear?" Mom asked.

An excerpt from *Henry Heckelbeck Chills Out*